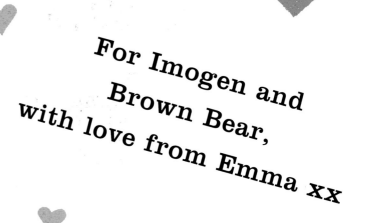

For Indie,
with love, Giles

For Imogen and
Brown Bear,
with love from Emma xx

ORCHARD BOOKS

338 Euston Road, London NW1 3BH

Orchard Books Australia

Level 17/207 Kent Street, Sydney, NSW 2000

First published in 2014 by Orchard Books

ISBN 978 1 40832 749 4

A CIP catalogue record for this book

is available from the British Library.

1 3 5 7 9 10 8 6 4 2

Printed in China

Orchard Books is a division

of Hachette Children's Books,

an Hachette UK Company.

www.hachette.co.uk

I love you baby

Giles Andreae & Emma Dodd

ORCHARD

Guess what I've got? Hip hip hooray!

A brand new baby to love all day!

Aren't I lucky? Yes, I know!

Why don't you come and say hello?

One fat tummy, tight like a drum.

Two little cheeks on one little bum!

Two little arms, and under the vest,

One little neck and a soft, warm chest.

Two chubby legs and two squashy thighs.

One little forehead, two round eyes.

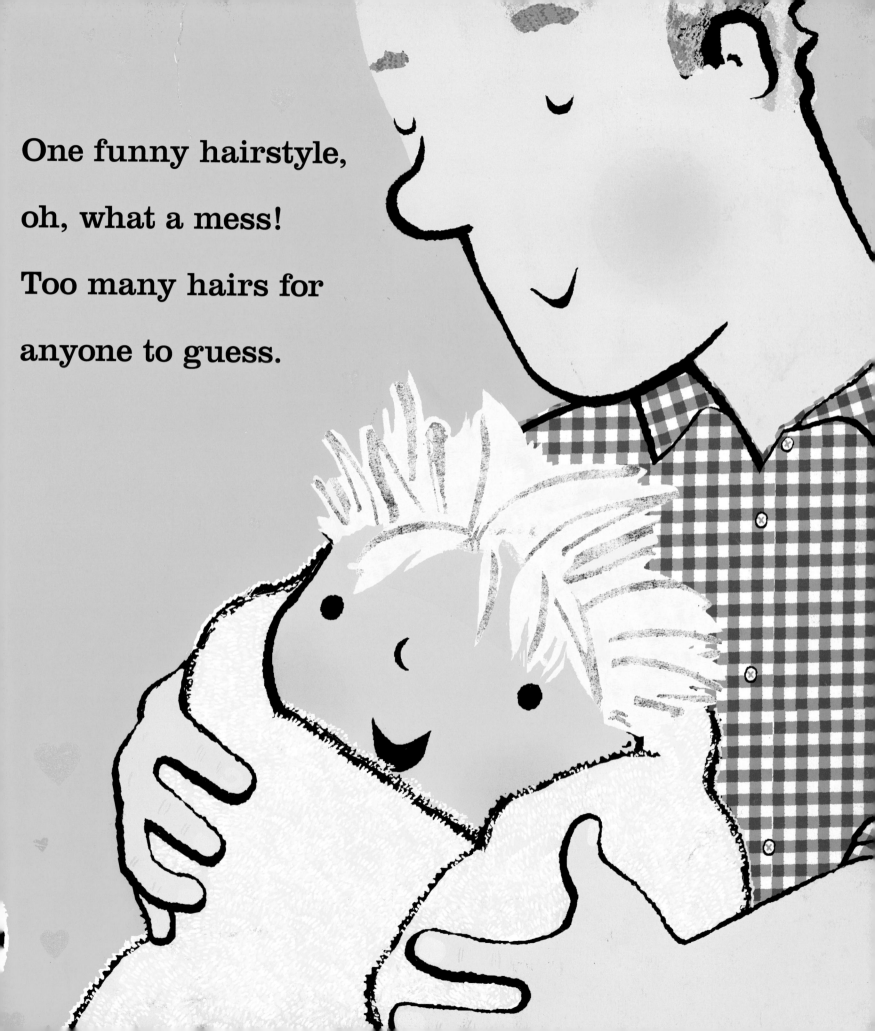

One funny hairstyle,
oh, what a mess!
Too many hairs for
anyone to guess.

Two tiny hands and
one small chin,

Eight squidgy knuckles

with dimples in.

Two strong shoulders,

two little wrists.

Two plump knees,

now, what have I missed?

One squishy waist and two tubby hips,

One kissy mouth with two soft lips.

Just one belly button, small and sweet,

Two pudgy ankles, two tickly feet!

Ten little fingers, ten little toes,

Two little ears and one little nose.

Two warm cheeks, all rosy and bright,

A kiss and a cuddle to say goodnight.

One sleepy face on

one sweet head,

Sleep tight, love you,
it's time for bed!

what